For my Old MacMother, with love
—S.L.J.

To Captain Keith and Starboard Bob
—J.N.

By

Sally Lloyd-Jones

ILLUSTRATED BY

Jill Newton

HARPER BLESSINGS

HarperCollins*Publishers*

Old MacNoah built an ark, **Ee-i-ee-i-o**.
And for that ark he got some wood, **Ee-i-ee-i-o**.

With a **BANG! BANG!** here
And a **BANG! BANG!** there,
Here a **BANG!** There a **BANG!**
Everywhere a **BANG! BANG!**

Old MacNoah built an ark, **Ee-i-ee-i-o**.

And on that ark he had two cows, **Ee-i-ee-i-o**.

With a **MOO! MOO!** here

And a **MOO! MOO!** there,

Here a **MOO!** There a **MOO!**
Everywhere a **MOO! MOO!**

Old MacNoah had an ark,

Ee-i-ee-i-o.

And on that ark he had two ducks, **Ee-i-ee-i-o**.

With a
QUACK! QUACK!
here

And a
QUACK! QUACK!
there,

Here a **QUACK!** There a **QUACK!**
Everywhere a **QUACK! QUACK!**

Old MacNoah had an ark, **Ee-i-ee-i-o**.

And on that ark he had two pigs, **Ee-i-ee-i-o**.

With an OINK! OINK! here

And an OINK! OINK! there,

Here an OINK!

There an OINK!

Everywhere an OINK! OINK!

Old MacNoah had an ark,
Ee-i-ee-i-o.

And on that ark they had some rain, **Ee-i-ee-i-o**.

With a **SPLISH! SPLASH!** here
And a **SPLISH! SPLASH!** there,
Here a **SPLISH!** There a **SPLASH!**
Everywhere a **SPLISH! SPLASH!**

Old MacNoah had an ark, **Ee-i-ee-i-o.**

And on that ark they had some lunch, **Ee-i-ee-i-o**.

With a **BURP!**
SLURP! here

And a **BURP! SLURP!** there,

Here a **BURP!**

There a **SLURP!**

Everywhere a
BURP! SLURP!

Old MacNoah
had an ark,
Ee-i-ee-i-o.

And on that ark it got quite smelly, **Ee-i-ee-i-o**.

With a
POO! POO! here

And a
POO! POO! there,

Here a **POO!**

There a **POO!**

Everywhere a **POO! POO!**

Old MacNoah had an ark, **Ee-i-ee-i-o.**

And on that ark it got quite rough, Ee-i-ee-i-o.

With an **OOPSIE-DAISY!** here

And an **OOPSIE-DAISY!** there,

Here an **OOPSIE!** There a **DAISY!**

Everywhere an **OOPSIE-DAISY!**

Old MacNoah had an ark, **Ee-i-ee-i-o**.

And from that ark they saw dry land,
Ee-i-ee-i-o.

With a **YA-HOO!** here
And a **YA-HOO!** there,
Here a **YA!** There a **HOO!**
Everywhere a **YA-HOO!**

Old MacNoah had an ark, **Ee-i-ee-i-o**.

And no more ark now, here's the end, **Ee-i-ee-i-o**.

With a
BANG! BANG!
here

...A SPLISH! SPLASH!
there

Old MacNoah had an ark,

Ee-i-ee-i-o!

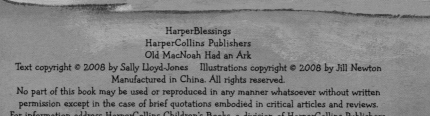

HarperBlessings
HarperCollins Publishers
Old MacNoah Had an Ark

For information address HarperCollins Children's Books, a division of HarperCollins Publishers,
10 East 53rd Street, New York, NY 10022. www.harpercollinschildrens.com

Library of Congress Cataloging-in-Publication Data
Lloyd-Jones, Sally.   Old MacNoah had an ark / by Sally Lloyd-Jones ; illustrated by Jill Newton.— 1st ed.   p.   cm.
Summary: After building his ark and loading it with animals, Old MacNoah must deal with mealtimes and their aftermath on the high seas.
ISBN-10: 0-06-055717-6 (trade bdg.) — ISBN-13: 978-0-06-055717-1 (trade bdg.)
ISBN-10: 0-06-055718-4 (lib. bdg.) — ISBN-13: 978-0-06-055718-8 (lib. bdg.)
[1. Animals—Fiction. 2. Boats and boating—Fiction. 3. Stories in rhyme.] I. Newton, Jill, 1964– ill. II. Title.
PZ8.3.J7538Old 2008   2006000342   [E]—dc22   CIP   AC

Typography by Carla Weise   11 12 13 SCP 05 04 03 02   ❖   First Edition